I just wanted to thank you
for reading my first book.
It was a long time coming-
sometimes painful-and like a
proud father-I'm hopeful it will
mature and make a difference
along the way.
I would appreciate your com-
ments, and be happy to speak at
your group or book club.
Please consider submitting a
review on Amazon.com and
"Forever Changed" for your
next gift! www.way.org

mac mcConnell

FOREVER

CHANGED

A Journey in Jericho

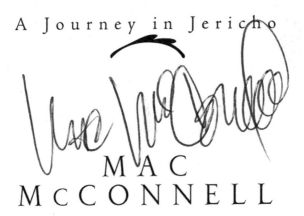

M A C
McCONNELL

WINEPRESS **WP** PUBLISHING

WinePress Publishing (PO Box 428, Enumclaw, WA 98022) functions only as book publisher. As such, the ultimate design, content, editorial accuracy, and views expressed or implied in this work are those of the author.

ISBN 1-57921-857-1
Library of Congress Catalog Card Number: 2006925575

One Way Productions—www.way.org—(954) 680-9095
Printed in Korea

DEDICATION

With great joy I dedicate this first book to my Mom and my Dad. They encouraged me to be me and then said they were proud of me, and I'm proud to be called their son.

DEDICATION

It is never too late for change.
No change,
no life.
What a waste.

TABLE OF CONTENTS

THANKS

My greatest model of achievement, perseverance, unbridled enthusiasm, and unwarranted favor comes from my wife, Linda. She conducts her life with great character and motivation, never expecting more of others than from herself. When she says, "You can do it, Mac; you can do anything," I realize she believes in me. And I hate to let her down. Thanks for marrying me—again.

Also, thanks to Richard Cannon, my personal change agent, Dr. Richard Hinners (1952–2002), a master of communication, and Mike Jeffries, champion of dashes, commas, jots, and tittles.

This story would not be possible without a very special gentleman, Dr. Phil Hoskins, a model of selflessness (see Special Mention).

PREFACE

I will apologize up front. This read may be cumbersome at first. It reflects a cumbersome life. A life in jolts and spurts, reverses and second guesses. Not unlike life itself. But a great excuse to wonder . . . I could have, I should have, I would have, or just plain why not? Thanks for taking the journey—enjoy.

My life as a dramatist forces me—if not coerces me—to look at life through the eyes of the characters I portray. Therein lies the very basic secret of characterization. Often the veneer of reality is all too transparent. The benefit is to learn the whys of behavior and discover new perceptions previously conceived as one-dimensional personalities. Taking anybody at face value is dumb. More importantly, boring. I hate it when I am treated on first impression. I'm just not sharp enough to be "on" all the time. I want folks to get to know me. You know, the interesting stuff, which may be buried a bit. So, I have decided there is a lot to learn, or at least to be amused at, by imagining what it would be like to be, well—just about anybody—no matter how dead, for how long. History will repeat itself, they keep telling us, unless we learn from it. I am not a history buff. I am a character buff. And it is easy to forget that legendary figures had real lives. Way too often we pigeonhole them in very small boxes, forgetting they are, like us, complex, with heartaches, joys, failures, successes, even bad breath, or are just having a bad day.

This journey in Jericho herein unwraps attitudes totally real. Reactions too personal to ignore. Doubt all too tangible. And yet to identify, when opportunity comes, no matter how late in life, it can change anything—everything. Someone wiser than I (which may be a long list) said, "The epitome of stupidity is doing the same thing over and over expecting different results." There is a little of each of us in each of us, or as it has been coined to death, "it takes one to know one." How we ultimately manage the balance may determine the amount of caterpillar or butterfly that emerges, or not.

Mac McConnell

ONE
A Little Too Little

The most horrifying event of my life
to date.

I could not have,
    would not have,
ever thought.
But Father said,
       "Your mother is dead."

I was all of six years old.

I was told I would soon have a brother
       or sister.
But instead,
I lost my mother.

This was Father's way of explaining things.

So, most of the time, I had the house to myself after
    Torah school.
To myself, and Hadie,
      the aunt.
She was all the mother I knew, and I was more than
    pretty sure she was a prostitute.
I became suspicious after I started school.
She had "company" every time I came home.

Now, I'm ready to retire.
     No wife, no kids,
and the territory is growing.
Folks scared silly of the government I represent.
I'm over, in charge of, all the other tax collectors.
Although I have to watch my back.
I have money stashed all over the house and under
    the house.
     Don't trust banks.
Besides, they would know how much I make, and
    that is none of their business.
     Nobody's business.

It's time to hire someone.
Someone to take over.

A Little Too Little

No,
someone to buy me out.
Even better.
        Yes, that's it.

Another day, another denarius.
I may be short, but the shekels pile up.
The richest man in town.
Well . . . probably.
Certainly the best dressed,
        probably.

Same old story for twenty years.
I have a routine.
I like routine.
I know what I am going to do and when.
When
things changed.
        And so had I.

Hard to explain what happened.
Still a mystery.
Had no idea I would change.
Had no idea I needed a change.
No idea I wanted a change.
        No idea.

Just tending to business like my father told me.
  Like he taught me.

I had given very serious thought to becoming a
  Talmud scholar.
Went through Bet-Sefer and Bet-Talmud. But, Father
  made fun of the whole thing. Called me a sissy
  when I wanted to study Torah instead of playing
  with Nat and Izzy.

I was a little too little to compete with the likes of
  them.

They would hide.
Then throw rocks and laugh as I ran to the house to
  escape behind the slam-of-the-door.
Only to hear that ungodly noise and laughing from
  Aunt Hadie and the "company."
    Or catch them in the act.

I knew what they were doing.
They knew I knew and would toss me my hush-
  money before Father got home.

I saved the money.
Father knew nothing.

A Little Too Little

I'm sure.
     I thought.

This was my world. My room. My money.
Mine. All mine.

I shined and counted it every day.
My money.
Didn't spend it. Not much.
Couldn't spend it. Not much.
Father would find out. If he found out, he would
     confiscate my stash or cut off my allowance.
So I hid things.
Trinkets and rings.
They were beautiful.
Someday I would have lots to polish,
     and count,
          and show off.
It made me feel big.
     Bigger.
I may be short, but the shekels pile up.
And someday I'll be the big man in town.

Squirt.

Father's favorite name for me. Squirt. I would just
    smile and think
        I'd like to squirt him.
But, his belt was always too handy and he would
    use it anywhere,
        anytime.

Soon I found out that if I wanted to save my hide,
    my pride—what little was left of each—I'd better
    behave in public. Besides, he was gone all day
    and Aunt Hadie would let me do most anything
    as long as I was on lookout for her.

Someday I'll get a harlot.
I have money.
I have plenty of money, and the harlots are every-
    where.

I talked to them on my way home from school.
    They were nice to me. Giggled a lot. Wore lots
    of pretty bangles.
They would talk to me until some of their "com-
    pany" came by.
They all knew Aunt Hadie.
They always asked about her, but they sounded silly
    when they did.

"How's Haaadie doing these days?" There was a tone
in their voice, but they never came right out and
said anything.
I knew.
Of course I knew.
I could add this up.
      Didn't take a wise man to add this up.
They knew her because she was just like them. But
they were the ones nice to me, and so as far as
I was concerned, what they did was their busi-
ness.

Hadie's company was nice to me too if they knew
what was good for them.
All I had to do was give them a look and here came
my payoff.

They bought my silence cheap,
      at first.
But when I saw them at market or temple, the cost
of silence became dear.

Amazing.
So many men would come through our doors for an
hour or so and leave to go about their business as
if they had just stopped by for a midday meal.

In just a few short years I knew them all.
I knew more about them than they thought.
I knew more about them than they wanted me to
     know.
          I knew more about them than I wanted to
               know.

Some of the company I saw at temple every
     Shabbat.
They would cover their faces when they saw me
     see them.
Cover their faces or look away.
"Do you know him?" Father asked.
"Who? Know who?"
"You know who, he hid his face from you?"
"No sir," I would say.
          But I did.
Now, there I was lying in the temple.
But I knew my little lie was nothing compared to
     theirs.

All the priests knew me well.
I studied diligently while in Bet-Talmud. Near the
     top of my class. There was even some serious
     posturing with my father to have me become one

of their Talmidim disciples. Many of the rabbis in town earned sizable stipends for mentoring would-be rabbis.

I wanted desperately to be a rabbi.
To be respected.
Tall or short. No issue to a rabbi.

All eyes were on the rabbis as they offered incense and prayers and blessings from Jehovah Elohim.
They had respect.
They commanded respect.

They were heads and shoulders taller than everyone when they stood on the regal lectern and held Torah.
Torah was holy.
The temple was holy,
and so were they.

I could not wait for Shabbat.
When I was old enough to sit in the lower gallery, I could worm my way up to the front.
Close enough to kiss the altar.

My prize, my tallit.
Regal and grand and holy. I would draw it up over
  my head, just to the edge of my phylactery, with
  great reverence for all to see.
      No one would see.
But just in case,
I was careful to observe all the ceremony.
I would kiss each side of my prayer shawl and bow
  and rock and pray.
And I was in another world.
I would close my eyes to imagine I was ten feet
  tall.
I would squeeze them hard, not wishing reality to
  steal back in.
The scent of incense delighted my nostrils.
I could smell heaven itself as I sucked in the aroma
  of prayers lifted high
      as my tears drizzled out,
          and down.
The stench of life, as seen by a tiny boy constantly
  covered in the dust of Jericho roads, now re-
  placed with fragrance of reverence in this holy
  place.

My tallit would absorb these wondrous aromas and
  ooze them back to me for the whole week.
My very own tallit since bar mitzvah.

TWO
Bar Mitzvah

A grand day in the life of a Jewish boy.
A holy day in the life of a Jew.
With many, the only holy day in the life of a Jew.
I wanted to be holy.
      Surely this day would make me holy.

Mostly I remember Nathan.
Like a reed he was.
Like a reed that shot up overnight.
Just for my Bar Mitzvah.
On my Bar Mitzvah he goes and grows.
I could only ask, "Why-do-we-have-to-be-Bar-
    Mitzvah-TOGETHER?"
Not fair. I was so much wiser.
He so much taller.
I would have worn stilts, but would surely fall and
    everyone think I was a fool.

So, I determined to be first that day in my recitations
    and readings of Torah.
No.
He should go first, and I could show him up.
It was the best decision.
     I was sure.

Then it began.
The time was near. I knew, and it started.
Little beads at first.
Then they started to drool.
To drip.
Over my eyebrows.
Down my cheeks.
I was shvitzing. Sweating.
All I could think was
my tallit would get soaked.
Torah would get soaked.

The chatter in the temple was deafening.
I was trembling and shvitzing.
I wanted to cover my ears and scream.

Then the hush.
     A holy hush.

Bar Mitzvah

Rabbi Shatim held his hands high toward heaven to
    begin the daily prayers.

My time was near.

I looked at Nathan.
      Nathan?
I looked again.
      His face?
Fear had washed his face.
He looked putrid.
He looked like he'd seen Elijah.
I was amazed,
      and I was glad.

Nathan was always so sure of himself, but now
    he looked like a frightened lamb ready for the
    slaughter. I think I saw him twitching, and
    something told me
I was going to be fine.
      Just fine.

I looked up at Father and he was smiling.
Smiling.
Smiling at me.

I can't remember the last time my father smiled at
    me. Laughed maybe.

He placed his hand on my head, on my tallit, then I
    saw surprise had scrunched his brow.
He cocked his right eye up high and eyed my
    tallit.
        The tallit.
I suddenly remembered this tallit, my tallit, he had
    not seen. The one he got for me was so ordinary,
    and I took some of my fortune and exchanged it
    for the most beautiful tallit in Jericho.
But Father had not seen it.
        Until now.
I had forgotten.
I was trembling,
        again.

But, Father squatted down to whisper a prayer in
    my ear.
A prayer.
I had to look to make sure this was my father.
He had not prayed with me for . . .
        I could not remember.

His hand, now gentle, and sliding ever so slightly to
    the back of my head, and pulling close to kiss
    my cheek.
I felt tears.
    Tears.
I felt his tears.
His tears rolling down my face. And I began to weep
    with him.
"I'm proud of you, my boy."
        "I'm proud of you, my boy."
                "I'm proud of you . . ."
His hand on my shoulder now.
He stood
        and heaven itself rested on my shoulders.
        And I was smiling.
My face drenched.
I was ready.
This must be what it feels like to be holy.

I have little memory of what happened next.
A blur.
A warm blur.
I was numb.
As I returned to stand with my father, there was so
    much commotion and chatter.

Loud, but distant
and muffled,
as I basked in the glow of thunderous applause
and blessings
and hands on my head
and kisses on my cheeks,
and I don't know what
all.
I even got a look from Marisha.
And the glow spread to my face, my smile.
I must have been very good.

As we left the temple, two rabbis rushed and
approached my father.
They huddled.
Father was nodding and thanking them and
smiling.
"I'll give it some thought," he said, "I'll give it some
thought."
Then he placed his hand on my shoulders and ush-
ered me along. His hand was not gentle anymore,
and I heard him under his breath as we left for
home to rest on Shabbat.
"They just want our money, my son.
You did well, but schooling is over."

Bar Mitzvah

And the glow was too.
He was not going to give it some thought.
I went to my room.
I knelt by my bed.
I folded my beautiful tallit.
I pulled it to my face.
Drank in the smell.

I placed it on the shelf and pretended to close holy
doors that existed in my mind.
I placed my yarmulke on top and draped everything
with a purple sash I had bought for this very
purpose.
I stared and wondered, *Will I ever go back to
temple?*

It was a long day, and somehow I was glad
it was over.

THREE
A New Tax Collector in Town

One day
the thunder of chariots startled everyone in the
    market.
        Everyone stepped back.
Roman chariots.
Clouds of dust and dirt billowing behind them as
    they roared through the marketplace to the
    magistrate's home.
        Zadok's home.

There were three chariots with three horses for each
    and two huge Roman soldiers in each chariot.
    People and goats and dogs scattered away from
    the roadway as they choked back their horses,
    grinding to a halt.
        The chariots stopped.
            Soldiers stepped off.
                Dust swirled around them.
They were magnificent.

But there was trouble.

The centurion pounded on the door and barked,
"Open."
I was surprised the magistrate was not already at
the door.
We all were surprised.
We all heard them.
Everyone heard them coming.

At once an officer ran to the back of the house,
snagged Zadok and reappeared with his prey
thrashing about,
gasping for air.
Grasping for help.
No one helped.

The soldier's hand clinched the throat of the man
as he dragged him around to the front of the
house.
The first officer drew his short sword.
In one motion he slashed Zadok nearly in half.
Blood gushed on the centurion
and the ground,
and the magistrate slumped.
The soldier released his grasp.

A New Tax Collector in Town

Fight and life was pouring out.
Zadok was dead as he hit the ground
       face down
              with a thud.

Gasps were heard throughout the crowd.
We were frightened.
We backed up.
Closed in.
Hoping to hide behind each other.

All happened so fast.
All too stunned to run.
       I looked away,
hoping it wasn't happening.
But I could not take my eyes off the dead man.
I was only thirteen—had not seen a killing.
Death, yes.
       Killing, no.

The officer scraped the blood off right on the
    magistrate's tunic and rescabbarded his sword.
He kicked him.
       No response.
Then the officer whirled around and started walk-
    ing toward me, toward the crowd, and everyone

backed up, scurrying away, and tripping and
    falling down.
"Be still," he roared. "Witness the justice of Rome
    when you attempt to cheat the Emperor. You,
    and you, and you—tend our horses. Now."
The officer summoned three lads as they left for the
    market and some ale.

I watched as they strutted to the bar.
I looked back at the body in the dirt.

Zadok was not only the magistrate but also Jericho's
    tax collector.
Father said he was a scoundrel
and a cheat
        and a traitor
                and a bum
                        and on and on.

Father hated Zadok.
The whole town did.

One day,
some time ago,
        Father had explained.

"Son, Zadok makes his fortune from cheating the citizens. Rome pays him to collect taxes, and he's free to add on his take. The taxes were small at first, then every year there was more and more. First it was the poll tax; the tax on our income. Then came the ground tax on all property. Just for good measure, Quirinius added a census, or head tax, so he could keep track of the poll and ground taxes. If a merchant dealt in barter, then the taxes were on his produce, grain, wine, and fruit. Soon, merchants were paying taxes on what they grew and sold and what they bartered for. They were taxed on taxes."

Father was getting hotter by the minute.

"Then on top of that, with all the nerve, they imposed a road tax on roads they did not even build."

Father got up to pour some wine.

"You know," Father started up again, "the pass from Jerusalem to here is the only way in and out or through, so they have you coming and going. No one gets in or out without paying that stupid road tax. Now with the Jerusalem road so treacherous with robbers, I'd just as soon get robbed by the thieves than the tax collectors. Both would leave you to die when they got their money."

I left the room, went out back to the latrine.
I was certain my father was about to start throwing stuff that I would have to duck.
And then clean it up.
I came back.
It was as if I never left.
Father was cursing as I entered.

"That swine Zadok was honest enough at first. Even crusaded for the job, though no one else would want it. The people here are good people, and Zadok was once one of us. Always at temple. Always spending his money. Generous with waiting on his taxes when folks were in a jam or the harvest was late. Then Rome increased the tax, he said. Have to charge more, he said. And, he changed. More demanding. Instead of allowing time for the taxes, he started calling them loans so he could charge interest.

"Then the parties began. Harlots would go in the front door while others went out the back. Merchants were supplying him with food and drink, and he would pay them with our hard-earned money."

I wanted to go to bed.
"Are you listening, boy?"
     It would be a long night.

Father spit. "Somebody's going to cut his throat
    someday."

Someday arrived.
That day.
With the Romans.

So,
I was shocked.
Of course I was shocked.
Father approached the centurions. He had no taste
    for Romans.
But there he was crossing over to the drinking hole
    and ordering a round for the soldiers.
My eyes bulged.
I could not believe what I was seeing.
Then I feared Father had a dagger and was going to
    kill himself a Roman.
Even worse, everyone else saw it too.

Everyone was staring. Hoping Father was going to
    kill himself a Roman.

Then my father came back.

"I think I've got the job, son."
"Job? What job? You have a job already."
"Tax collector." Father was grinning.
He was joking?
        But he wasn't laughing.
"No, Father, you hate them, the town hates them,
    everyone hates them."
"I'll be fair and the people will be glad."
"No, they . . ."
"Enough. It's done. We're going home."

I couldn't hold my head up.
Trying to hide all the way home at the edge of
    town.
I was afraid everyone would know and they would
    talk about us behind our backs
and wish we were dead.

All I could think,
I'm too little to have a tax collector for a father.

FOUR
I Should Have Been a Priest

I would have been a priest.
I could have been a priest.
And I regret not continuing my education.
Father let me return to Bet-Talmud the year after
    my Bar Mitzvah.
        I begged him every day.
This was a must before becoming a Talmidim for
    any rabbi.
It was a safe environment.
It would distance me from being known as the tax
    collector's son.

I was enchanted by everything.
My own world.
My escape.
Mine.

Soon I had students of my own as they began Bet-
    Sefer, as I had when I was six years old.

To them I was ancient when I celebrated my
 fourteenth birthday.
I was a man at school. The big man at school.
 And loved to teach.

The first day was the best.
They would come in and sit quietly, not knowing
 what to expect.
This was a special day and a well-kept secret.
I will never forget my first day in school,
 and would make sure they would not forget
 theirs.

I would stand just inside the door of our little school-
 room as each little one skittered by.
Many would try slipping in.
Startled to find me standing there, peering down in
 my full regalia. They would not have their prayer
 shawls as yet. Not until their Bar Mitzvah. And
 at their age, just as I was at their age,
intrigued at its beauty and meaning.

As they took their seats in a semi-circle two rows
 deep, I would imitate Rabbi Shatim.
Walking ever so slowly by the first row, looking
 down my prominent nose.

I towered over these little ones and had my strut.
They would become perfectly still.
Not afraid.
      Not at ease.
And they were mine for the next five hours to teach
    and to tease.
I would turn my back and walk away—glance
    quickly back to their giggly response.

Then the moment began.

Just inside a small cupboard was the magical jar. I
      would open the door and reach in ever so care-
      fully, slowly.
Holding the suspense.
      Holding the prize.
I cloaked the jar under my tallit.
As I reached the first student on the first row, I un-
    veiled the well-known vessel.
      The well-known treasure.
Honey.
I had their attention now. Everyone knew what was
    in this jar.
It was reserved for very special occasions.
They could not believe their eyes.

I remembered well, for I could not believe mine on
my first day.

All Jewish children know they would enter
schooling.
This was not an option.
None expected to like it.
None expected such a treat the very first day.

I peeled back the wax seal.
The aroma escaped.
It filled the room and the little noses.

The back row, standing by this time and all their
little necks stretched to the fullest in hopes that
their noses were not lying to their eyes.

"Children."
"Yes, Rabbi." I had to laugh; I was a long way from
being a rabbi. But they would flatter me because
of the treat I held in my hands.
"Not a rabbi, my little ones, just your teacher for
now. Take your slate."
"Yes, Teacher."

They scurried to sit and reach under their little
benches and grab their slates.

There was urgency.
>   Eagerness.
I looked carefully at each to see if there was but a
>   hint any one of them knew what was coming.
No.
The secret was secure.
"Children."
"Yes, Teacher."
Would you like some honey?"
"Yes, Teacher."
It was a beautiful chorus. I would be their best friend
>   today, if not for a long time.
"Dip your finger into the jar."
"Yes, Teacher."

My last three classes were all the same, for I was
>   holding a true treasure, and they would be
>   very obedient until they had the honey on their
>   tongue.
>   That was the point after all.
"Now, spread the honey on your slate."
"Yes, Teacher."
Honey to my ears.
"Now lick the honey from your slate."
Not a sound.
They looked to see if I had lost my mind.

But only for a moment, then they were at it.

Slurping every last remnant of honey.

I would watch with such joy.

They would lick the slate with such joy.

They licked their hands,

then the slate,

then their lips.

And then they would look to see if there was more.

Then they would rest their little slates on their little laps and look at me. Hoping against hope that I had another wonderful surprise for them their first day of school.

I did.

More wonderful than honey, only they may not realize it at the time.

"Children."

"Yes, Teacher."

Anticipation swept their faces and spread their eyes.

I reached for a scroll.

The only sound was the beautiful rustle of the ancient parchment as I unrolled to the prophet's words and told them;

"Remember the words of the prophet Ezekiel,

'Then He said to me, Son of man, eat this scroll I am
    giving you and fill your stomach with it.
So I ate it, and it tasted as sweet as honey in my
    mouth.'"[1]

"Children."
"Yes, Teacher."
"Remember the words of the psalmist,
'Taste and see that the Lord is good; Blessed is the
    man who takes refuge in him.'[2]

"Children."
"Yes, Teacher."
"The Lord is the lover of your soul. His words are
    more precious than gold, than much pure gold;
    they are sweeter than honey, than honey from
    the comb."
"Yes, Teacher."

Some would understand.
All would learn every word of Torah for the next
    four years. The very first taste of Torah would be
    the most wonderful taste of honey. The words
    of our people, of our life would be sweet as the
    honeycomb. They would never think of honey
    without thinking of Torah. They would not think

of Torah without thinking of honey. Each would make them want the other. Soon they would be the same. Honey–Torah. Torah–honey.

Each day they would eagerly write on their slates. The same slates where the honey had been. They would remember.
          They would taste.

I would dictate.
They would write.
"Read it back, children."
"Yes, Teacher."
They did.
"Children, clean the slate."
"Yes, Teacher."
They did.
"Now recite."
They did.

I would dictate.
They would write.
"Children, clean the slate."
"Yes, Teacher"

"Now recite."
They did.

I would dictate.

"In the beginning God created the heavens and the earth."[3]

They would write,

then erase.

"Recite, my children."

"In the beginning God created the heavens and the earth."[3]

"Very good, children. Now write. 'The earth was formless and void, and darkness was over the surface.'"[4]

They would write.

They would read it back, clean their slates, and recite.

Then the most important first test.

"Now, children, all of it together."

There was a moment of fear.

A moment of quiet.

They began.

"In the beginning God created the heavens and the earth. The earth was formless and void, and darkness was over the surface."[5]

"Very, very good, children."

And so we would begin the amazing journey of the
    history of our people.
Dictate
Write
Read
Clean
Recite.

Dictate
Write
Read
Clean
Recite.

Then each eve of Shabbat,
before time to leave, I would test them.
I would give them a scripture, and they would give
    me the ones before and after.
They would learn the words
and the whys,
       and they were good.

Their reward was a piece of honeycomb for the best
    student.
Many times all would receive some honeycomb.
I was easy.

I Should Have Been a Priest

They were proud of themselves
      and I was too.

A faint memory now, although a good one.
I should have been a rabbi . . .
      I would have been a rabbi . . .

      I could have . . .

FIVE

"Working Today?"

I dismissed my little ones early one day.
I was not well at all.
My throat was raw.
My nose was stuffed.
What wasn't clogged was dripping.
My attitude was ungodly.
I was about to faint.
Best to spare them my wrath and shoo them on
home.

Their parents would be cross with me for the unexpected—unwanted intrusion into their routine.
But Rabbi Shatim was nowhere to be found to
step in,
in my absence.

I went home pondering, "Should I do this the rest
of my life?"
I loved teaching and loved my little students.

I was good at this.
Better than good.
       Very good.
I was respected.
My height was perfect.
       Nearly perfect.
Not too tall for the little ones and not too short, as
    not to be taken seriously.
The income would be very respectable when I fin-
    ished my formal training in four more years.
    Then, my internship the next six years would
    gain me a seat on the lower council.
Then,
       in at least a hundred more years
I could be considered to be chief priest.
That was my heart's desire.
Away from my father.
Away from the stigma as a tax collector's son.
Respect.
       And, Chief Priests were exempt from the
         tax.
That's respect.

But, I think you really have to be holy for that job.

I reached my home.

"Working Today?"

I reached for the door.
I heard an all-too-familiar sound from my house.
"Hadie, I told you no more."
I was sick, and I was mad.

The back door slammed, and I thought, "Good rid-
    dance, now I'll get some rest."
But, I entered my room and saw what I saw out of
    my window . . .
an all too familiar figure.
Rabbi Shatim.
No!
            Yes.
                        It was.
I sank to my knees.
My chin hit my chest.
I shut my eyes but could not shut out the sight.

Rabbi Shatim scurrying away, with Hadie running
    in the opposite direction.
The godly.
The ungodly.
            Now the same.

Father came home late that day.

The sun was setting
as I was sitting,
        waiting.
"How's business today?" I asked, not looking.
"Taxing," Father said with his chuckle.
The same reply with the same grin.
I gave my same reply.
        Nothing.

Father had changed this last year.
New roof.
New addition to the house.
Our food delivered now.
No more trips to market, and I missed them.
But with all the looks and sneers, it was best.

Folks, at first, got used to the idea of the new tax
    collector, but then Father took up more and
    more of Zadok's habits.
I had taken the roundabout way to temple each
    day.
I thought it best.
Most must have known I didn't approve of my
    father's business.
Most must have known I could do nothing about
    it.

Most would not know what I was thinking
now.

"Is that a new moneybag?" Of course it was. I had
not seen it before.
"Yes, look, two secret compartments I had special
made. You like it?"
"Are you working tomorrow?"
"Yes, of course. Why?" Father's voice sounded an-
noyed that I asked such a stupid question.
"Can I . . . come with you?"
"You? Yes, of course. Why?" This must have sound-
ed more stupid.
"I'm through with temple. Through with school.
Through."
"About time," Father said.
"Let's celebrate my son. Honeycomb?"
"No . . . ,
yes . . . ,
why not?"

SIX
Why Not?

Two words would change my life.
Why not?
Not the wisest choice for deciding my future, but
the only one I had at the time.

Father woke me.
"Boy, it's time."
"Time? Time for what?"
"Time to get up. You're going with me; this is a tax-
ing day. Have you forgotten so soon?"
I had.
"Are you coming?"
"Why not."
A statement, not a question.
I got dressed and ready.
Out to the latrine and back to grab some fruit.
We left.

Father must have wanted some company; he was actually civil with me and let me sit on the donkey with the new moneybag just in front.

It was fine leather.

I wondered how much money was in there.

Father would not trust the bank, and I assumed he had good reason. And would certainly not leave much, if any, in the house with both of us gone.

I sat on a woven burlap blanket, which began to itch immediately.

We went through the town, past the baker.

"Good morning, Jared," Father said.

Jared looked up and barely waved a floured hand.

We passed the blacksmith.

"Good morning, Rufus."

Rufus pushed the huge bellows with a grunt as embers released a shower of sparks.

Father was silent from then on, glancing back at times to see if I was awake.

My tuckus already sore.

I knew it would ache all night and the next day.
      And maybe the next.

Father saw me grimace.

Why Not?

"Relax your muscles, son, it will help."
It didn't.
    That was our conversation.

Father led the donkey through a narrow pass to a
    little valley with a small settlement of homes
    and farms.
Father stopped.
He looked through a patch of bushes. We had come
    all the way around to the far side of the village.
    We could see the homes, but they were not in
    sight of each other.
I felt a tremor of fear as we started up again nearing
    the first home. I had never gone with Father to
    collect taxes before and had no idea of what to
    expect.
Father stopped again.
He turned and reached for me.
I did not plan this.
Before I knew it, Father lifted me and set me to the
    ground. For the first time, I realized I was as
    tall as he.
    Which was not tall at all.

We were many yards from the house and could just
    see it through the scrub of trees.

Father was going to leave me here because he
    expected trouble.
"Boy, go see if anyone is in the house."
"What?
Why?
Me?"
"Yes, just go and knock and call out to see if anyone
    is in the house."
My stomach lurched.
"Then what? What if no one is there?
What if there is?"
These were my questions.
"Not to worry, just go."

Father was pushing with his hand on my back; my
    resistance was useless.
        His belt too handy.

I slipped along the edge of the trees, looking every-
    where for signs of life.
Hoping to find none.
There were some farmers off in the distance but a
    slight stream of smoke was coming from the
    chimney.
Someone was home—so I turned to go back—only
    to bump into Father.

Why Not?

He was right behind me.

"Go on," he said in a whisper behind a finger up to his lips.

I was confused.

But no choice.

I took the one step onto the porch and looked at the door.

I looked back to Father.

Needing a way out of this.

   Wanting a way out of this.

This was worse than Bar Mitzvah.

He held up his fist and knocked the air, and I knew to knock on the door.

I did.

Nothing.

I looked at Father again.

He held up his hands and cupped them to his mouth, so I called out, "Hello."

But, my voice cracked and nothing came out.

I cleared my throat, "Hello."

I heard steps.

I stepped back.

The door opened and there was a big man holding a cup, wiping schmutz from his beard.

It was lunchtime.

"Well now, young fellow, what do you . . .?"
Then another voice.
"Good day, Ezra."
It was Father.
He appeared from the side of the house.
Ezra was surprised.
I was surprised.
        And glad.
"Be right back," was all Ezra said.
He was right back.
With a small bag of coins and counted out eight
    denarii.
Ezra closed the door with a thump.

It came to me.
It was simple.
And it worked.
Just the way father had planned it.
I was his shill.
I was embarrassed.
I was relieved.
It worked.
        Oh no.

"Perfect," Father said and turned toward our
    donkey.

Why Not?

I started after him.
"Perfect," he said again.
He was smiling.
Then he said something amazing.
"Good job."
He said good job.
> And this was a good sound.

"One down and nine to go."
"Nine to go? I have to do this again?"
> This was not a good sound.

"Nine more agains. Of course. You saw how it went.
Perfect."

I knew he was right.
But I didn't think I had one more in me,
much less nine.
The first time I didn't understand.
Now I did.
And I was scared.

We went back to the road and turned toward town,
and I thought Father had changed his mind and
we were going home.
> But no.

He turned and we went back behind the line of trees
till we approached another home.

I knew this time.

"Go."

Was all the instruction I was given.

I wanted to go.

Home.

Anywhere.

This was frightening.

"Go, I'll be right behind you."

There was that tone.

No choice.

I went.

But kept looking back to see Father shooing me
along.

I knocked.

Door opened.

"Hello young man, what . . ."

"Morning, Mara."

"Oh, you startled me. Has it been thirty days?"

"You know it has."

Father's tone was firm, and Mara turned and left
and came back. She had a handful of coins.
She handed them out, but they dropped to the
ground.

"Sorry," Mara said, as she closed the door hard.

"Get those, boy."

Why Not?

Father was already leaving as I reached down to
    collect my first tax dollars.
As I picked them up, I blew the dirt from them and
    just stared.
Money.
I like money.
And here I was holding a handful.
        It felt good.
I had helped, and it felt good.
"Eight more to go, son, good job. This will be the
    earliest I have completed this route and we will
    celebrate tonight."
All I could think was, *How am I going to ride that
    donkey home with my sore tush?*
"Boy, you could get used to this."
"They will know next time, Father."
"Next time is thirty days. We have fifteen other
    routes that don't know a thing."
We.
Father said *we* have fifteen routes.

"You said *we* have fifteen routes."
"I said we. Welcome to the life of a tax collector.
    You're good and will be very good. I have a
    feeling."

I didn't know what to say.
I didn't have anything to say.
>Then I said,
"Father, why did we go to the end and work back-
wards?"
"So they wouldn't spread the word or see us coming.
I change every time or they will keep the doors
locked or go to the fields. You have to know
these people and their habits, but today we really
threw them. Before you know it, you will have
routes of your own."
"And a donkey?"
"And a donkey. And two denarii a route."
I just looked at father to make sure.
"Two a route."
"That's what I said boy."
This would be fine.
>Just fine.

It wasn't long till I had my own routes.
It wasn't long till it was three denarii a route.
And it wasn't long till I learned some tricks of my
own.
Some days I would wear a hat. Some days I would
start in the middle of the route and crisscross.

Why Not?

Sometimes I would ride my donkey right up to
the house, and some days I would throw stones
on the roof.
It was a game.
A serious game.
And I was good.
     And getting rich.

Then Father started having parties and drinking, and
     there were prostitutes now, and the prostitutes
     pinched my cheeks and patted me on my tush,
     and they laughed.
Father would look
and wink.

One day a young one came into my room.
I paid her.
Father never called me boy again.

SEVEN
Money Talks

Father fell off the donkey one day, dead.

It had been fifteen years since I had joined this
business.
His business.
He just fell off the donkey one day.
Dead.
Mourners were bought and paid for.
Harlots joined the funeral processions or it would
have been a short one.
Father had expanded the territory. Had six tax col-
lectors reporting in.
Father taught me to keep a close eye on them.
To go on their routes from time to time.
To keep things honest.
Honest?
Nothing honest about this business.
But Father was the chief tax collector and respon-
sible to Rome for all the taxes in three regions.

69

Now my regions.
It was expected.
Father told Centurion Varian the last time he came
    to collect the books,
and to take the loot to Jarius,
that I would be taking over soon.
Soon came.

There was a Roman outpost in Jericho now, with
    a squadron of soldiers and money to spend.
    Jericho's market district had more bars and more
    business and more harlots.
More taxes.
I had more parties and more harlots.
My friends were tax collectors.
Harlots.
And anybody I bought from.

Money talks in this town.
       And I spoke very loudly.

With the Roman soldiers in town, no one gave me
    any trouble.
But I didn't travel alone after dark.

Money Talks

I was supervisor, chief among the tax collectors, and didn't need to travel at all if I didn't want to.

EIGHT
Four Stops to Make This Day

Father had been dead four and a half years when we
    first heard about the miracle man. The Romans
    talked about him and laughed or just sneered.
        I was busy.

I didn't bother much with temple, not for a long
    time.
I respected Shabbat when I remembered, and cel-
    ebrated Rosh Hashanah, and Yom Kippur on
    my own.
        If at all.
But rabbis were talking plenty.
They talked to me because I paid the temple tax at
    Passover, and I was generous.
        Which made things right.

I asked them about this miracle man.
"They say he has Talmidim and draws a crowd and
    performs wondrous things."

"Who?"

"Yeshua from Nazareth."

"They say? Who says?" I asked.

"The centurions. Romans and traveling merchants
and the gypsies say."

"What do you say?" I asked.

"I say, we say, he's a charlatan."

"Have you seen him?"

"No, but, we listen."

"You listen and you talk."

I had heard about this Yeshua.

I heard about them all.

My experience with the religious lot told me to trust
no one.

Besides I was set.

       I thought.

Rubin left town.

Just up and left.

I told Yoseph to cover his route. He said he could
not take on anymore.

I was surprised.

Yoseph was ambitious and seldom turned down
more work.

He had gambling debts.
So, I had no choice.
Must keep things current.

I got Rubin's book and saw it was time to collect his
    route. It had been some time since I had worked
    this route.
        Any route.
I was not delighted.
I checked the book and saw there were four stops
    this day.
So I dusted off my pouch.
I locked my house and went to get my donkey.
        He looked at me like I was a stranger.
                I was.
But, off we went.
Through town,
past the market,
past the old baker.
"Good morning, Jared."
He smiled.
        He'd better.
I was a very good customer.
I passed the blacksmith.
I had not been through town in some time.
He looked at me and that was all.

I came to the first appointment.
The man Bartimaeus.
I could not believe I was calling on Bartimaeus.
 The blind man who begs in the street.
This was actually in Rubin's book?
But he had collected taxes from him. At least that is
 what the record said.
I walked up to the door and I knocked.
Nothing.
I knocked again.
I shouted.
"It's Zacchaeus, the tax collector. I need to see the
 master of this house,
for the taxes are due this day."

I had no shame.
That was gone long ago.
I'm Zacchaeus, the chief tax collector, and no one
 hides from me.

Bartimaeus opens the door.
His hands waving in front of him as if feeling for
 trouble.
His eyes glazed,
full of pus, and I looked away.

I had avoided him in town, at the gate, in the
    street.
But often,
at least sometimes,
at least once in awhile,
dropped a coin in his cup.

I'm thinking, *Why am I here, wasting my time?*
"Yes, Mr. Zacchaeus, I know who you are. I am the
    master of this house, and I know my taxes are
    due."
"So, where . . ."
"But, you know me, and you know that I am blind
    and cannot work like other men. That govern-
    ment that you represent refuses to give me an
    exemption."
        Rubin must have been doing his job.
"I'm afraid that I do not have your tax money to-
    day. But I promise you, if you could give me
    mercy . . . for . . . thirty days, I will get your
    money."

Thirty days.
The familiar scheme.
The route was every thirty days, and he knew I
    would not resist the extension.

I could have demanded a deed to his property, al-
though I didn't really want this property.
But I could have.
I should have.
I would have.
But, I didn't.
I just turned to leave.
Then turned to remind him,
"I will be back in thirty days; your debt must be
paid."

This was not starting off to be a good day in the
tax-collecting business.

I checked my book and could see the next appointment was just a few steps away.

This was not the best part of town.
I thought about taking an indirect approach, but it
had been a long time since I had this route, so I
walked right up to the door.
I knocked on the door.
I knocked again.
Nothing.
Perfect.

The first one blind.
This one deaf.
I shouted.
"It's Zacchaeus, the tax collector. I must see the
     master of this house, for the taxes are due this
     day."

Then out of the darkness of the house, into the light
     of the doorway, came an awful sight.
Is this a man?
Is this a woman?
I wasn't sure if whatever, whoever, it was, was going
     to make it to the door at all.

It was a woman.
But her skin was all yellow.
Her face was all pale.
She coughed and coughed and coughed into her
     shawl.
It was disgusting.
I was going to vomit.
I'm thinking *I should call the undertaker* when,
"Yes, Mr. Zacchaeus, I know who you are."
Everybody knows who I am.
"And I know my taxes are due." Cough, cough.

"But, sir, I have an incurable blood disease, and
    soon I will die." Cough, cough, cough, gag. "Mr.
    Zacchaeus, the physicians have taken all of my
    money." Cough, gag, cough. "But they've done
    nothing for me. I'm afraid I don't have your
    taxes today, but I promise," cough, cough, "if
    you will show me mercy," cough, cough, "for
    just thirty days," cough, gag, cough, "I will get
    your money."

I'm thinking, "Thirty days?
She won't last thirty days.
What if she dies, then what am I suppose to do?
I have every right to confiscate her belongings."
I could have,
    I should have,
        I would have,
but, I didn't.
I just turned to leave.
But I turned to remind her,
"I will be back in thirty days. Your debt must be
    paid."

A knot in my stomach.
Two in a row.

Four Stops to Make This Day

I have lost my touch.
I checked Rubin's book again.
    But no delinquencies noted.

Next stop just around the bend.
    I stopped.
        I peered around a tree.
There were three scrawny little kids sitting outside
    on the porch,
wearing rags for clothes.
Someone must be at this house.
They would not leave these little ones alone.

I walked up.
    They looked skinny and pitiful.
Streaks running down their dirty little faces.
    They must have been crying.
I asked them,
"Where is the master of this house?"

Just then, their mother came to the door.
She too was wearing rags for clothes.
    She too looked skinny and pitiful.
I could tell by the dark circles around her eyes
it had been a long time since she had had a decent
    night's sleep.

I could tell by the bruises on her arms and on her
    neck,
something was very wrong in this house.

Then I heard a disgusting, ugly, scary noise out back
    of the house.
I looked around that lady, and I saw . . .
a man
running around in circles.
And he was wearing . . .
nothing.
He was naked.
And he was screaming at the top of his lungs. And
    . . . and he was gouging at his flesh with a sharp
    stick
when that lady . . .
"Shhhhh, shhhhhh."
She clutched her rag of a robe up around her throat
    and waved her hand in front of her face for me
    to be quiet.
That was fine with me.
       I was ready to run for cover.
That man could take me apart.
"Mister, be quiet, what do you want?"
She was whispering and shaking all over.

"I'm Zacchaeus," I whispered back, thinking I
     should just go now.
"I'm the chief tax collector. I must see the master of
     this house. The taxes are due this day."

I got too loud.

"Shhhhh. Mr. Zacchaeus, I am the master of this
     house. That is my husband, you see. He is pos-
     sessed by demons from another world. No man
     has been able to chain him. No man has been
     able to bind him, and certainly no man has
     been able to tame him. Sir, he has not been able
     to hold a job for more than a few hours. Mr.
     Zacchaeus, it takes all I can make or scrape to
     care for my precious little children. I'm afraid
     I don't have your tax money. But if you could
     show me mercy for just thirty days, I can get
     your money."

I stood there staring.
This is not the way it is supposed to be.
All these people had learned the same drivel.
Mercy.
     Thirty days.
          They have figured something out.

Who is she kidding?
Thirty days?
She will need thirty days just to clean those scrawny
    kids and get away from that madman.
I should just go get my cart and drag it down here
    and empty out that house before that no-count
    husband ruins everything.
I could have.
    I should have.
        I would have.

But, I didn't.
I just turned to get my donkey and get out of there,
    yelling over my shoulder.
"I will be back in thirty days. Your debt must be
    paid."

This has been a terrible day in the tax-collecting
    business.
What will I report to Jarius?
      Nothing to report.
So I will not report.
Not for thirty days.
    I'd better just call it a day.

Four Stops to Make This Day

Why, if word of this day gets out to my other tax
        collectors . . .
I have a reputation.
I'd better cut my losses and head for the house.

But, my next stop is only a few steps away.
Just down the way.
Back toward town,
so, why not?
            After all, it could not possibly be as bad as
                these.

I walked to the door.
I knocked on the door.
It opened, and there stood a woman;
no!
In black.
            Not a good sign.
"Yes, Mr. Zacchaeus, it's my taxes. They are due, I
        know."
Finally, easy pickings, I'm sure.
"But, Mr. Zacchaeus, you know me."
"I do?"
"Yes, and you know I am a widow."
"I do?"

"Yes, and as you can see there is a funeral here
  today."
"I can?"
      I did.
"It's my only child, my boy is dead."
Now what?
"Sir, the funeral man has taken all my money for the
  funeral expenses."
      Here it comes.
"I'm afraid . . ."
"Let me guess. You don't have your tax money."
"Yes, I mean no, I don't. But—and I have never asked
  before—if you could show me . . ."
"Mercy for thirty days?"
"Yes, I will have your money."

This is a nightmare.
The worst day in my tax-collecting career.
This is the kind of day that makes me wonder if I
  ought to look for a real job.
Naaaah.

It was a long walk home that day.

At least my donkey wanted to go home and dragged
  me for a change.
I had to slip off the roadway several times to avoid
  being seen.
I told the donkey, "This is just between you and
  me."
No reply.
Long walk home.

  And a longer thirty days.

NINE
Thirty Days Passed By

I traveled to Cyprus, by the Jordan, to kill some time
    and drown my predicament.
A popular haunt for the likes of me.
Wine.
Women.
Lots of tax collectors.

I was practically famous here.
A good place to spend my money where the people
    of Jericho would never know.
        Not that they would miss me.

I rented a room for thirty days.
Would go to the tavern.
        For thirty days.
I talked about everything.
Everything except that route.
But no one was listening.
The topic of conversation was this,

this man Yeshua.

"Yes," I said, "I have heard of him."
Wild tales were circulating, and everybody added
    their two mites worth.
Healer, they called him.
        Miracle worker, they called him.
            Turned water into wine, they said.
Five loaves into a banquet, they said.

"He's in Jericho the last I heard. Did you see him,
    Zacchaeus?" asked the barmaid.
"Do you see me?
Am I not here?
Am I in Jericho?"

Perfect, something finally happens in Jericho and
    I'm here.

"Josh, another round."

The only miracle I need is someone to take that
    forsaken route off my hands.
No one gave it a thought.
I bribed.
I threatened.

Thirty Days Passed By

I wasted my time.
No takers.
     They knew,
         no doubt.

That's why Rubin left in the middle of the night.
Just before tax day.

I could not wait any longer.
The report was due and that route had no report.
None I could report.

I went back to Jericho.
Thirty days was here.

It was a dreary day that day in Jericho.
Something told me this would be a big waste of
    time.
But, I got my book,
my pouch,
my donkey,
     and I got going.
I passed the baker, the blacksmith.
"Why don't you get a respectable job?" he said.
"Like being a blacksmith?

That's real glamorous."

He puffed his bellows, banged his anvil,
sending a shiver down my spine.

I didn't even try to hide.
What a waste.
I came up to my first appointment.
Blind Bartimaeus.
I should just forget this altogether.
But, here I was.
I knocked on the door . . .
      and . . .
a rather handsome-looking man came to the door.
He had a smile on his face.
I wasn't sure who this was.
And real sure he didn't know who I was.
     I don't get many smiles in my business.
I thought I'd better introduce myself.
"Shalom, my name is Zacchaeus. I'm the chief tax
    collector in these parts. I need to see the master
    of this house, for the taxes are due this day."
I showed him my book for proof.
"I'm the master of this house."
"You? I don't think so."
     This was a joke, a ploy, a mistake.

"The last time I was here, the master of this house
    was broke. Didn't have two shekels to rub
    together and had no prospects because of his
    blindness."

He was still smiling. Even more.

"That's right. But I am the master of this house.
    And you were right about my being broke. And
    right that I had no prospects because of my
    blindness.
But, I'm not blind anymore."

"Wha, wha, what did you say? Not blind any-
    more?"

I didn't like the sound of this; this was a trick of
    some kind.
"I don't think I understand."
    I was getting steamed.
"You better just explain yourself right now."

"Calm down, Mr. Zacchaeus. As a matter of fact,
    I've been looking forward to a chance to tell you
    about the greatest day in my life. Yes sir, I was
    blind and broke, no prospects, lost everything,

almost my hope, except, my friends told me there was a man named Yeshua in town."

"Who?"

The name sounded more than familiar.

I knew who.

"Yeshua. They said he was performing many miracles."

"So?"

"I knew I needed a miracle."

He was right about that if he thought this story would help his taxes.

"So, I made my way to the edge of town. I plopped myself down right outside the city gate and waited for Yeshua to pass by."

"How would you know?"

I thought this was a good question.

"I heard a crowd coming. I got to my feet. I yelled, 'Yeshua, Son of David, have mercy on me.'"

More mercy.

At least not from me this time.

"Then what happened?" He had my attention at least.

"The crowd pushed me back. I felt an elbow in my ribs. There was a hand on my shoulder, pulling me. I felt men crowding in front of me. They told me to shut up, get back, go away."

"And?" I was curious at least.

"I could not shut up. I would not get back. I yelled again. Louder this time. 'Yeshua, Son of David, have mercy on me.'"

"And?"

"And someone said, 'He's calling for you.'"

"Then?" Why was I standing here listening to this?

    Why was he talking to me?

       I told him who I was.

          I just needed my taxes so I could go on.

But he went on.

"The man who gripped my cloak was trying to stop me, but I just slipped out of that coat. I left it and made my way to Yeshua. I felt my way by touching, pushing through the people. Suddenly they were pulling me forward, when I heard his voice.

'What do you want of me?'

"It was Yeshua talking to me. It must be. 'Master, healer, you have the power to cure me of my blindness.'"

"Then?" This man could tell a good story at least.

"He just said, 'Your faith has healed you, go in
    peace.'"
"And?"
"It was like a fog cleared from my eyes. I could see.
    I could see the man. The healer. He was smiling.
    Then he turned, and the crowd followed. And
    so did I. All day and into the night. Then I came
    home. My friends were there; they had heard,
    and they were glad."

This man was grinning.
I was stunned.
Is this true?

"Mr. Zacchaeus, I can see. I'm not blind anymore.
    I've been able to see ever since that day. I have
    my life back. You know, that's not all of it. Truth
    is, I have new life ever since the day Yeshua
    passed by."

"What about my mon—?"
"Yes, I have found work, and I have your taxes." He
    reached for a bag on the shelf by the door.
He handed the bag to me.
"Go in peace. I sure hope you meet Yeshua someday.
    When he passes by."

Thirty Days Passed By

I was dumbfounded.
I was dreaming.
Nobody had been this happy to pay their taxes
    before.
He was beaming. It was Bartimaeus. I could see. And
    he could see.
I was beaming.
I was a happy man.
I was happy for him,
maybe a little jealous.
Maybe I can meet this Yeshua someday.
        But not today.
            I have work to do.

I backed away from the house.
I opened the bag and looked in.
The money was all there, all right.
I shoved it into my satchel and left.
I looked at my donkey to make sure I was in the
    right place.
To make sure I was in my right mind.
My head was swimming.
Bartimaeus could see.
He found work.
He paid his taxes.

I hurried on down the road.

I checked my book.
>   My next appointment just a few steps
>   away.
But, this lady is probably dead by now.
But, I walked up to the house.
I waited.
I knocked.
I heard someone walking.
The door opened, and . . .
a lovely-looking lady was standing there.
With . . .
>   with a smile on her face.

I wasn't sure who this might be.
And I was sure she didn't know who I was.
I don't get a lot of smiles from ladies.
Harlots yes,
>   ladies no.

I thought I'd better introduce myself.
"Shalom, my name is Zacchaeus, I'm the chief tax
    collector in these parts, and I need to see the
    master of this house, for the taxes are due this
    day."

"Shalom, shalom, Mr. Zacchaeus, I am the master of this house."
"Wha, wha, what did you say?"
She was about to giggle.
"What do you mean you are the master of this house?"

She was just standing and smiling.

"Why, the last time I was at this house the master of this house was half dead.
I didn't even expect she would live thirty days.
I didn't even expect to see her again.
Just who are you?
Am I at the right house?" I thought this was a good question.

"Yes, you are at the right house, Mr. Zacchaeus."
Now she was giggling.
"I am the master of this house. And I have been looking forward to a chance to tell you about the greatest day in my life."

I don't remember anyone looking forward to telling me anything.
Except how much my bar tab was.
I'm in a daze.

"You are right, Mr. Zacchaeus. I was half dead. I
   didn't expect to live even until this day. My
   condition was worse. The physicians had taken
   all my money and they had given up, given me
   nothing but a death sentence."

"And?" I couldn't wait to hear this. I looked around
   to see who might have put her up to this, when
   she said,

"And I heard that there was a man named Yeshua
   in town."

This must be a conspiracy, is all I could think.

"I had heard of the man. I had heard of his ministry.
   I had heard of his miracles. And I knew I needed
   a miracle."

It's a miracle I'm still standing here, is all I could
   think.

"So?"

"So, there was a crowd coming down my way. I
   heard them. I heard a boy calling to his friends,
   'It's Yeshua, it's Yeshua.' Mr. Zacchaeus, it took
   all my strength to make my way down to the
   street. And then when I got there, the crowd,

there were so many. I could not get to Yeshua. I could barely see him. I could not reach him. I thought, *If I could just touch him—just his clothes—I would be healed.* With all my strength I stretched my hand out. I fell. But as I fell, I touched the hem of his garment. And instantly, I knew I was healed. I felt the health rushing through my body. My face could barely contain my smile. My heart could barely contain my joy. I was healed."

I was stunned.
I looked around again to see who was pulling a prank.

There was no one.

"Mr. Zacchaeus."
I looked back.
She had touched my arm.
It was a soft and gentle touch.
I looked at her face.
It was soft and gentle.
She was still smiling.
There was a gleam in her eye.
Softness all over her face.

No woman—no nice woman—had looked at me
    like this.
Or touched me like this.

"Sir, it's as if I never had a disease at all. I have my
    life back after twelve years of dying. And that's
    not all of it. Truth is, I have new life, ever since
    the day that Yeshua passed by."

I was staring.

"And, you know what else?"
I didn't.
I didn't know anything.

"I don't have anymore doctor bills, and I have your
    tax money."

My jaw hit my chin as she turned and picked up a
    small purse and counted out eight denarii and
    placed them in my hand.
I stared at the coins.
I stared at her.
I stared at the coins.
"Mr. Zacchaeus, go in peace. I sure hope you meet
    Yeshua when he passes by."

Thirty Days Passed By

My mouth was hanging open.
I probably looked pretty stupid.
The next thing you know, I'll start believing in
    miracles.
But whatever had happened to her, I know this,
       I have my money.
Much to my surprise, I have my money.
Maybe I can meet this Yeshua someday.
But not this day.
       I have appointments.
Not a good idea to miss my very own appoint-
    ments.
I backed away from the house.
I wasn't sure which way to go. I wasn't sure what
    was happening.
But this was no prank.
       The money now safely in my satchel.

I checked my book.
My next stop was just down a piece.
I snatched the rope holding my donkey and headed
    down the road.

Here we are.
The door is closed.

No children that I could see.
I stopped and listened.
I remembered.
Wouldn't want to surprise a madman.
I didn't hear anything, so I hurried right up to the
     house.
I knocked on the door.
It opened right away.
What is this?

That woman that was here before came to the
     door.
Wearing a . . .
brand
               new
                         dress.
And, there's a smile on her face.
I guess so, with a brand new dress bought with my
     tax money.
She is not real bright.
Or didn't know I was coming.
And didn't even look to see who was at the door.
Then,
     her little children came to the door.
They didn't look pitiful anymore.
And . . .

and, they had on brand new little outfits.
And they were laughing
and giggling.
And their little tummies were full,
and their little faces were clean.

And I wondered where the party
or the rich uncle was
when, a rather stately-looking stranger came to the
     door.
Then, he put his arm around that woman's
     shoulder.
Then, she slipped her hand around his waist,
and I was thinking, *Well, would you just look at
     this?*
*She must have gone and gotten herself a new
     husband.*
And that was good.
Because she needed one
          real bad.
Then she looked at me.
     Smiling.
"Good morning, Mr. Zacchaeus, we've been expect-
     ing you."

"Expecting me?"

I was shocked.
Nobody expects me
and opens the door
      too.
And certainly not with a smile on their face.

"Yes, we want to tell you about the greatest day in
    our lives."

Greatest day?
This is the strangest day of my life, and everybody
    wants to tell me about their greatest.

"Mr. Zacchaeus, do you see what has happened to
    my family in just thirty days?" She looked up at
    that man and then knelt to hug her children.
Then she stood up.
She looked right at me.
"Sir, I owe you an apology."

Shocked again.
Apology?
Never had an apology.
    From a debtor.
She looked back at her husband and put her arm up
    around his shoulder.

"When you were here before, I told you that my
    poor husband was possessed by demons from
    another world. That no man could bind him.
    That no man could chain him."
 She looked back at me. "And certainly no man
    could tame him. But that was before we met that
    miracle-working man named Yeshua."

There were tears in her eyes.

And . . . and I think my eyes were getting watery.
I must be catching something.

"You see, sir, I heard that Yeshua was in town. I
    prayed to God that he would come down my
    street, and he did. But when he stopped outside
    of my house, my husband came running right
    at the crowd. Right at Yeshua. My husband was
    ranting, and raving, and growling, and pitching a
    fit and shouting curses, and falling to the ground,
    and stirring up a cloud of dust, and everyone
    backed up. Suddenly Yeshua shouted.
'Spirit, be quiet.' And everyone got quiet."
And she continued,
"My husband jerked, fell on his back, then just fell
    all limp. But, then he opened his eyes. He got

up. He walked right over to Yeshua. Yeshua was smiling. Yeshua took his outer robe and gave it to my husband. My husband put it on. Then he threw his arms around Yeshua. Yeshua threw his arms around my husband. Then—sir—my husband came right up to the house and he hugged me. 'I'm so sorry,' he said, and then he hugged me again.

"Do you see, Mr. Zacchaeus? I have myself a brand new husband. Do you see sir, my children have themselves a brand new daddy, and we have our life back?"

Then that man spoke to me.
"That's not all of it, Mr. Zacchaeus. Truth is we have new life. All because Yeshua passed by. And something else, sir. I've been able to hold onto my job, and we have your tax money. Go in peace. We sure hope someday you too can meet Yeshua when he passes by."

Now I was smiling too.
I had lots to smile about.
What a day.

Thirty Days Passed By

My bag was full.
Why, this was the best day in my tax-collecting
    career.
When word of this gets out,
the other tax collectors will think I'm a genius.
I was thinking,
I should just call it a day.
I'm three for three.
Why tempt fate?
       I will just head for the house.

But,
I checked my book.
The next stop was just a few steps away,
right on my way home, just across the street,
       so why not?

I walked up to that house.
I started to knock on that door,
but something inside was saying to me,
Maybe you're not the mean old tax collector you think
    you are.

I started to knock on that door,
but something inside was saying to me,
Maybe there is more to life—than death and taxes.

I started to knock on that door,
but something inside was saying to me,
"Remember how you taught others to love their
neighbors."

I started to knock on that door, but something was
saying . . .
"Who are you, mister?"

I turned to look, and the door had come open.
There was a little boy standing there.
My hand was still in the air about to knock when
he said again,
"Mister. Who are you, mister?"
"Who am I? Who are you?"
"Oh, my name is Zoë; it means life. What is your
name?"
"My name is Zacchaeus.
That's Mr. Zacchaeus to you."
"What does your name mean, Mr. Zackus?"
"I said, it's Zacchaeus,
Mr. Zacchaeus.
It means "Pure Israelite.""
"Are you pure, Mr. Zack?"
"I said, it's Zacchaeus.
And that is none of your business.

Besides who are you and what are you doing here?
    The last time I was here the widow woman was
    burying her only son; he was dead."
        I'm thinking, *she left town and someone else*
        has moved in,
            and I had just ruined a perfect day.

"That's right, Mr. Zack.
I'm that boy. I was dead. But I'm not dead any-
    more.

Mr. Zack? Mr. Zack? Can you hear me?"

I fainted.
Completely.
Plopped right down on the porch.
I wasn't ready for this.
Why didn't I just go on home like I wanted to in
    the first place?

"Mister, are you all right?"
I sat up.
Then Zoë began.
"You want to hear about it, Mr. Zack? Maybe you
    better just keep your seat."
"It's Zaccha . . ., oh never mind, go on."

"Yessiree, I was dead. I was in the casket.

All my friends and family had come to mourn with my mom. We were in the funeral procession leading outside of town. But we met another procession. It was led by a Mr. Yeshua. Now the good part, Mr. Zack. This Mr. Yeshua heard all the commotion for my funeral. He saw my brokenhearted mom. He came right over to the casket and he saw me. But he didn't see death. He saw life. He took one look at that casket and said, 'Young man I say to you, arise.'

Before I knew it, my little heart was beating. Before I knew it, my little lungs were breathing, and out of the casket I came. It got real quiet for a minute, Mr. Zack. Then mom began shouting. I began shouting. The crowd began shouting. Mr. Yeshua began shouting. Everyone was shouting, 'Glory to God in the highest, he's not dead anymore.'

"Mr. Zack, the funeral man gave us our money back. Sir, the grave diggers said, 'No, no, this one is on the house.' Mr. Zack, we even have that tax-collecting fellow's money. If you see him, will you tell him we have his money? All because Yeshua passed by."

TEN

Guess Who's Coming to Dinner?

I was a little weak in my head.
I was a little weak in my stomach.
I was a little weak in my knees.
> But not too weak to see Yeshua.

I heard he was coming through town.
I forgot all about my tax money.
I ran to town as fast as my little legs could
carry me.
> My donkey was left in my dust.

I came to town, and there was a crowd around the
   man Yeshua.
A huge crowd.
Everyone was here.
But I was too short.
I pushed
and pushed
but could not get to Yeshua.

I jumped
and jumped
but could not even see Yeshua.

So I said to myself,
"I know what I will do.
I'll run ahead to the center of town and climb that
    old sycamore tree
and wait for Yeshua to pass by."
        I did.

I didn't have to wait long.
Before I knew it, there he was.
The crowd was following him, when he walked right
    up to my tree.
He stopped right underneath my limb.
I was sure he saw me, but he turned back to the
    crowd.

This is perfect.
I will hear everything.
I will see everything.
But, then,
Yeshua turned back and looked right at me
and started laughing.
I couldn't believe it.

Guess Who's Coming to Dinner?

He was laughing.
But it was different.
He wasn't laughing at me.
Not at all.
"Zacchaeus, come on down. Today I will come to
   your house."

"My, my, my house?"

It had gotten quiet.
All too quiet.
I climbed down out of that tree.
The crowd was staring.
I can't explain it.
I didn't care.
I invited Yeshua into my house.
        He came.
Just as he said he would.
I invited everyone.
They just stared.
Then they looked at each other.
I took off.
I started running toward my house.
I yelled at the baker.
I yelled at the merchants.
"Bring food. Bring drink.

We're having a banquet at my house
right now."
But then I saw the harlots and the other tax
    collectors.
They were coming too.
I didn't care.
        Yeshua was coming to my house.
Everyone was welcome.
Not everyone came.
I didn't care about that either.
There were smiles on everyone.
And I could not stop smiling myself.
There was much commotion and clatter and clang-
    ing of goblets and laughing and talking.
Yeshua was in my house.

"Zack, did you have a good day collecting taxes?"
Zack?
Yeshua called me Zack, just like that little boy.
But I didn't care. Not one bit.
"Zack, how's Bartimaeus these days? I heard he
    found work."
Yeshua was taking some bread and cheese and fruit,
    and he sat down on one of my cushions.
"Yes, very good day. Bartimaeus can see again," I
    blurted out.

"Yes, I know."
Yeshua started to eat, and his friends started to eat.
Respectable people.
Here, in my house.
"Did you meet my little friend Zoë?"
"Yes sir, I did. He's alive!"
I felt like a schoolboy.
"So I noticed." Yeshua said.

Yeshua said it without batting an eye.
When I realized he knew everything.
Everything about everything,
and everything about me.

"Sir."
"Yes, Zack, what is it?"
"I want to give half of everything I own to the
poor."
I could not believe what just came out of my mouth.
Apparently, everyone there could not believe
what just came out of my mouth, for suddenly
there was not a sound.
Everyone was staring at me.
Some froze with food falling out of their mouths.
Some had raised a goblet to their lips and stopped.
Someone was making a ruckus, but someone
shushed them.

"Are you sure, Zack?"
I guessed I was. I didn't give it a second thought.
"And, and, if I have cheated anyone, I will pay them
    back four times as much."
Now there were grunts and groans, and someone
    dropped their goblet with a thud and a clang.
And I knew what I was saying,
and it felt so good to be saying it.

"Good for you, Zack."

Yeshua stood to his feet and everyone looked at him,
    and it felt good they were not staring at me.
Then Yeshua, in a booming voice that sounded like
    all heaven broke loose,
"Today, salvation has come to this house."
        Silence.
Then thunderous applause.
I looked all around me and all were applauding as
    Yeshua came over and threw his arms around
    me
        and smothered me.

There were tears of joy in his eyes as he cupped my
    face with his leathered hands.
Two of his friends came, and before I could stop
    them they had hoisted me to their shoulders.

And everyone had started shouting and singing.
There was Bartimaeus coming in with his friends.
There was the woman who was healed.
And that family that have themselves a new man in
    the house.
And then little Zoë.
Zoë was laughing and dancing and singing and
    eating.
Everywhere I looked I saw people for the first time
    as friends and neighbors.
My friends and neighbors.

Yeshua gave me mercy.
My debt is paid.
I have my life back.
No,
      no,
          no,
that's not all of it;
      truth is,
I have new life.
And something else.
I, I am changed,
I am
      forever
          changed.

ENDNOTE

My life was very busy but not very full. My marriage a distant memory; my relationships forgettable. The fun that I crammed into the weekends was long forgotten long before the debt was paid.

There was a time I needed a change. I may not have known it. I may not have been exactly looking for it or thought I wanted it. It wasn't that my pants were dirty or my life so soiled. But I did realize I was headed nowhere in particular. Stuck in routine. Fortunately, like Zacchaeus, I had heard about this Yeshua. In fact, the evidence was everywhere, even overwhelming. Finally, I thought, *I'll just go check him out.*

It was in a little church. A soft-spoken pastor. But the message was loud and clear. That day Yeshua passed by my life. It wasn't the first time when I thought about it. But I wanted to make certain it wasn't the last time, for sure. I didn't give half of everything I had to the poor. Not that it would have amounted to much. I didn't rush to find out if I had cheated anybody and pay them back four times. That was a frightening thought. I did accept His salvation that day. My heart was renewed, my marriage restored, and my life changed, forever. It is huge yet simple. Basically encapsulated in the Gospel of John, chapter 3, verse 16. Check it out.

SPECIAL MENTION

The inspired ending of Zacchaeus's journey in Jericho began in the heart of Dr. Phil Hoskins, pastor of Higher Ground Baptist Church in Kingsport, Tennessee. He admits, "It may not have happened this way, but I bet you can't prove it didn't." This gentle giant readily said yes in 1999 when I asked to adapt his dramatic sermon into a one-man drama. This book would not be possible without his imaginative approach and selfless attitude. If you are anywhere near Kingsport, Tennessee, by all means, visit Higher Ground Baptist Church. You will be in for a change—maybe forever. It is located at 1625 Lynn Garden Drive, Kingsport, TN 37655, (423) 245-3141, or on the Web at www. HigherGround.org.

GLOSSARY

Bet-Sefer   First phase of Hebrew schooling.
                 Jewish children memorize To-
                 rah for approximately four years
                 beginning at age six.

Bet-Talmud   Second phase of Hebrew school-
                 ing. Jewish children memorize
                 all of Hebrew Scriptures from
                 Genesis through Malachi for ap-
                 proximately six years.

Jehovah Elohim   Lord God Almighty.

Phylactery   Small leather box holding parch-
                 ment of Hebrew Scripture placed
                 on forehead as reminder. An
                 amulet.

Tallit   Jewish prayer shawl.

Talmidim   Disciple, student, follower.

Torah   Pentateuch. First five books of
                 Hebrew Bible.

Tush, tuckas   The rear end. Butt.

Schmutz   Trash, scum, debris, dirt.

Shill   Swindler, con artist.

Yarmulke   Jewish skull cap.

NOTES

1. Ezekiel 3:3
2. Psalm 34:8
3. Genesis 1:1
4. Genesis 1:2
5. Genesis 1:1,2

Future Releases From
Mac McConnell

BOZRA
The Unprepared Shepherd
Proposed Release, March, 2007

HADAD
The Unsuspecting Innkeeper
Proposed Release, February, 2008

JOSEPH
The Unexpected Father
Proposed Release, December, 2008

NICODEMUS
A Crisis of Belief
Proposed Release, March, 2009

SIMON
After the Storm
Proposed Release, January, 2010

To order additional copies of

FOREVER

CHANGED

Have your credit card ready and call

Toll free: (877) 421-READ (7323)

or order online at: www.winepressbooks.com

Proceeds from book sales go to

One Way Productions, a non-profit corporation.

For more information:

Please visit www.way.org,

or call (954) 680-9095